THE
Mysterious Bender Bones

Weekly Reader Children's Book Club presents

THE

Mysterious Bender Bones

by Susan Meyers

illustrated by Ib Ohlsson

Doubleday & Company, Inc., Garden City, New York

Contents

THE
Mysterious Bender Bones

1

Worms for Sale

Kermit Fox and Brian Digby knelt beside the puppy run at the Belvedere Boxer Kennels. A fat brown puppy with a white streak down its nose and cropped ears still wrapped in bandages was eagerly licking Kermit's fingers through the wire mesh. "Atta boy, Flash," Kermit murmured. He had named the puppy the first day he saw him. "Just look at those eyes. You can see he's smart."

"He sure is a beauty," Brian said admiringly. "But fifty dollars? That's an awful lot of money. Where would you get it?"

Kermit sighed. That was the question he kept asking himself. Where was he, Kermit Fox, going to get fifty dollars? He stood up and tugged at the cowlick in his carrot-colored hair. He couldn't ask his parents for it. That was out of the question. Not that they wouldn't want him to have the puppy. In fact they agreed that a boy of Kermit's age should have a dog. But Mr. Fox was a college professor and probably didn't have fifty extra dollars. Even if he did, Kermit was certain he would never consider spending it on a dog—not when you could get one for free at the pound. He looked at Flash, who was wriggling and jumping against the wire mesh, and pulled even harder at his cowlick.

"You'll be bald before you get to high school if you go on like that, son."

Kermit stopped tugging at his hair and grinned a little sheepishly at Mr. Taylor, owner of the kennel. The man's own hair was thinning at the crown and Kermit wondered if he spoke from experience.

"You're the boy who was here last week, aren't you?" the man asked.

Kermit nodded.

Mr. Taylor smiled and leaned over the wire to pat Flash on the head. "I know what it's like," he said. "You see a pup like this and before you know it, you're in love. It's happened to me many times."

"No kidding!" Kermit looked at the kennel owner with new respect. That was exactly how it had been between him and Flash. He knew he could never be happy with any other dog. "Are they still fifty dollars?" he asked hopefully.

"Afraid so," Mr. Taylor replied. "Can't afford to go any lower, what with stud fees, and vet's bills, and all the food they eat." He saw the corners of Kermit's mouth turn down. "I know it sounds like a lot of money," he said apologetically. "But I'll tell you what I'll do. If you let me have twenty dollars now, the pup's yours. You can pay me the rest over the summer."

"Really, Mr. Taylor?" Kermit could hardly believe his ears. "Only twenty dollars?"

The kennel owner nodded. "That's what I said. Twenty now, the rest later."

"Gee, Brian, did you hear that? Twenty dollars! Could you hold him for me till I get it?"

"Well, I can't make any promises without some kind of guarantee, but I'll tell you what I will do. You write your phone number down here,"—he took a pad and pencil from his shirt pocket—"and I'll promise to call you if anyone else is interested in that pup."

"Gee, Mr. Taylor. Thanks." Kermit printed his name and phone number on the pad. "And don't worry. I'll be back," he said as he pulled Brian toward their bikes.

"Kids!" The kennel owner chuckled to himself as he watched Kermit and Brian race down the gravel drive. "What a pair!"

Kermit Fox and Brian Digby were quite a pair. Seeing them together always made people smile, for two boys could hardly look less alike. Brian had dark hair and tanned easily, while Kermit, with his carrottop, stayed red as a lobster all summer long. Kermit was tall and thin, while Brian was short and chubby. Though they saw each other only in the summer, when both their families rented bungalows in the Whaley Lake Summer Colony, they were still good friends. It was Kermit who thought up their wild schemes and Brian who brought him down to earth. At the moment, he was doing just that.

"I don't see what you're so excited about, Foxie," Brian objected, puffing a little from pedaling so hard. "Where do you think you're going to get twenty dollars?"

Kermit hated to be called Foxie, and Brian knew it. But this time he was thinking too hard to notice. "I've already got five dollars," he explained, thinking of the money he'd been saving for a new fishing rod. "So all I need is fifteen more. Now think. How are we going to get fifteen dollars . . . fast?"

"How are *we?* It's not me who's getting a dog," Brian grumbled. But it was Brian who suddenly came up with an idea. "Worms!" he exclaimed.

"Worms!" Kermit echoed. Why hadn't he thought of that! "Brian, you're a genius," he cried, stopping his bike. "A genuine five-star genius."

Brian stopped and polished an imaginary medal on his T shirt. "It was nothing, nothing at all," he said modestly.

"Worms," Kermit repeated. "Why, I'll bet we could sell hundreds. Thousands, even. Everyone at Whaley Lake goes fishing."

"They sell the big ones for a penny apiece over at Lake Carmel," Brian said. "I saw a sign there the other day."

A penny apiece. Kermit made some rapid calculations. Fifteen hundred worms at one cent each would make exactly fifteen dollars. The golden boxer puppy was just fifteen hundred worms away.

Brian was doing some arithmetic too. "Three thousand in all," he said after screwing up his eyes and biting hard on his tongue to imagine the numbers better. "That's an awful lot of worms to dig."

"Three thousand?" Kermit repeated. "But . . ."

"Fifteen dollars for you, and fifteen for me," Brian explained. "If we go into this together, we've got to share the profits."

Kermit groaned. Of course, Brian was right. But three thousand? It made him tired just thinking of digging so many worms. "Well, I guess we'd better get started." He sighed. "Let's put up a sign in Bigelow's General Store."

"Right," agreed Brian, hopping onto his bike. "Last one there has to buy the Cokes."

Bigelow's General Store was near the summer colony on the other side of the lake—almost six miles from the Belvedere Boxer Kennels. By the time Kermit and Brian dropped their bikes on the ground and staggered up to the Coke machine, they were too exhausted to argue about who had won the race. They put their dimes in the slot and sank down on the ground with the cool Coke bottles in their hands.

Only then did they notice Sergeant Toohill's black-and-white police car parked in front of the gas pumps. A plump little woman in a faded cotton dress was leaning on the front fender, talking a mile a minute and gesturing dramatically with her hands. The police officer's kindly face could be seen inside the car.

Kermit and Brian grinned at each other. "Let's see what Mrs. Bigelow's raving about this time,"

ian whispered. Taking their Cokes, they moved closer to the gas pumps.

"She came in yesterday. Just got off the train I'd guess from the suitcases and the way she was dressed. And she bought a shovel and a ladder and a rope and I don't know what all else . . ."

Mrs. Bigelow was the biggest gossip at Whaley Lake. Kermit wondered who she was talking about this time.

"Kept asking if anyone had been in here looking for her," the woman went on. "Acted very mysterious about the whole thing. Oh, she's crazier than ever, I tell you. Had that old cat of hers in a carrying case. Kept talking to him just as though he could understand. Titus. Always did think that was a peculiar name for a cat."

So that's who it is, Kermit thought. Mrs. Bender. Mrs. Bigelow never tired of talking about the woman who lived on the island. Bender Island. Kermit glanced across the lake to the long tree-covered strip of land in the middle. Through the trees, he could see the peaked roof and stone chimney of Mrs. Bender's old house.

"She's on her favorite subject," Brian whispered. "Boy, I sure get tired of hearing about old Mrs. Bender."

Kermit agreed. He didn't think there was anything so strange about having a cat named Titus —or spending the summer alone on an island. Of course, he had to admit that the island itself was not your usual run-of-the-mill island. You never knew when you'd run into a grimacing Japanese fudo or a Polynesian idol looking like he had the world's worst bellyache hidden among the trees. *Mr.* Bender, who'd died years ago, had been some kind of an explorer and, as far as Kermit could tell, he'd picked up just about everything in his path and shipped it home.

Mrs. Bender was hardly run-of-the-mill either. She wore enormous straw hats and dangling necklaces of shells and pumpkin seeds. But she let the kids swim off the big rocks at one end of her island, and sometimes she brought them cookies and lemonade. Kermit and Brian liked her.

"And that's not all," Mrs. Bigelow continued, but as she was about to begin another long story, the bell on the gas pump rang. Sergeant Toohill gave a little sigh of relief and noticed the boys for the first time. He winked broadly. "I guess the summer's officially started," he said. "You boys going into the detecting business again this year?"

Kermit squirmed under the police officer's grin.

He didn't exactly like to be reminded of that incident last summer, and for once he was glad when Mrs. Bigelow started talking again. "Let's go put up that sign," he said, and headed quickly for the store.

Sergeant Toohill would never let them live it down. And after all, it could have been a burglar breaking into the Simon's house that night. Then they would have been heroes for calling Sergeant Toohill. It wasn't their fault that it was only Mr. Simon who'd lost his key.

"He'll probably forget it by next summer," Brian said hopefully, as they stepped inside.

Bigelow's General Store was dark and cool. Everything the summer people could possibly want was crammed into one little room. The walls clear up to the ceiling were lined with shelves of canned goods, dry cereal, calamine lotion, and disposable diapers. There was a tempting display of fishing tackle and a glass case full of jackknives. But today, Kermit and Brian didn't linger over the knives and tackle as they usually did. They headed straight for the big bulletin board on the wall near the cash register.

Brian picked up a piece of paper Mrs. Bigelow kept handy by the board. "What shall we write?" he asked.

Kermit pulled at his cowlick and studied the other notices on the board. Someone had a used outboard motor for sale. Someone wanted to trade a pair of water skis for a guitar. And someone else was giving kittens away for free. But no one was selling worms. "Big, juicy, lively worms for sale," Kermit dictated. "One cent each. That should do it."

Brian printed the words neatly—or at least as neatly as he ever printed—on the paper and drew a big juicy-looking worm underneath. Then he tacked it to the bulletin board.

It looked good. The picture of the worm was eye catching, even if you couldn't tell right away what it was supposed to be. Still, Kermit wished he could think of some other way to earn money. It might take all summer to sell enough worms. He tugged at his cowlick for a few minutes and then it came to him.

Odd jobs. That would cover just about everything. He hastily printed, "Kermit Fox. Odd jobs done," on a slip of paper and tacked it up beside the worm sign.

"Uh, oh," whispered Brian. He nudged Kermit. Mrs. Bigelow had just come through the door. If they didn't want to spend the rest of the day talking about their families, their health, and how they had spent the winter, they would have to get out fast.

The plump little woman was just about to ask her first question, when Kermit and Brian streaked out the door. "So long, Mrs. Bigelow," Kermit called over his shoulder.

It was only a short distance from the store to the summer colony. Kermit and Brian turned their bikes off the main road and onto the dirt drive. The sign over the little road read *Whaley Lake Summer Colony*, but the paint was so faded that a stranger wouldn't have been able to make it out. The colony had seen better days. That was why they now advertised it as rustic, Kermit's mother said, but Kermit was glad no one had decided to improve it. As it was, there were no lawns to mow or hedges to clip.

The Digby bungalow was one of the first on the road. As they turned into the driveway, a shrill little voice called, "Brian!"

Brian groaned loudly as his five-year-old sister, Barbie, came running across the yard. "You've got to clean your room *this instant*," she announced when she reached the boys.

"Says who?" Brian grumbled.

"Brian!" Brian's mother called in an irritated tone of voice from the bungalow.

"That's who says so," Barbie replied, sounding pleased as punch. "Boy, is she mad at you!"

Brian groaned again and got off his bike. "Guess I've got to go," he sighed. "I'll try to get some worms dug later on."

Kermit gave him a sympathetic look. "O.K. See you tomorrow." He swung his bike around into the road. As he pedaled off he could hear Barbie's exclamations of delight. "Boy, are you going to get it, Brian. You're really going to get it."

"If I had a sister like that!" Kermit winced at the thought as he dug his shovel into the soft earth. Those books on child development that his mother was always reading said that the only child had all sorts of special problems, but Kermit didn't notice that he had any to compare with Brian's.

He surveyed the little yard around the Fox bungalow. It was lucky there was no lawn, because he figured he would have to dig up every inch of ground to get fifteen dollars' worth of worms. He bent over and pulled a worm from the dirt and dropped it into a coffee can. His back was beginning to ache and his hands were already sore from digging.

"Kermit, dinner's almost ready," Mrs. Fox called. "Come in and wash up."

Kermit dropped the shovel with a sigh of relief. He didn't usually like washing, but anything was better than digging. He felt so tired, he didn't even bother to count the worms he'd collected. He set the can on top of the table and turned the water on in the kitchen sink. Then he worked the soap into a lather and watched the dirty suds run down the drain. He could feel two blisters beginning to form on his hands.

"Are there worms in there?" Kermit's mother asked, eyeing the can suspiciously.

Kermit nodded.

"Well, then, I'd rather not have them on the kitchen table." Mrs. Fox set the can on the back step. "What are you going to do with so many?" she asked as she took a casserole from the oven.

Kermit mumbled something about fishing and was relieved that his mother was too busy getting the hot dish to the table to notice his reply. He didn't plan to mention Flash unless he absolutely had to. In fact, he didn't plan to mention anything about dogs until the puppy was actually his. That would take care of the possibility of any long discussions about the monetary value of boxer puppies. As far as Kermit was concerned, Flash was worth his weight in gold.

"Dinner's ready, Jim," Mrs. Fox announced.

Kermit's father put down his newspaper and came to the table. "Mmm, smells delicious," he said as he began to dish the meat from the casserole. "I've been reading such an interesting article, I didn't even notice it was dinnertime. It's about the late husband of our island neighbor, Mrs. Bender."

Kermit sat up and listened. He seemed to be hearing a lot about Mrs. Bender lately.

"Herbert Bender was a rather eccentric explorer and adventurer. I guess you know that. But it seems Bender was also something of an amateur anthropologist, and on his last trip to the Orient, he was lucky enough to find . . ."

"Jim!" Kermit's mother suddenly interrupted. "Look, there she is now."

Kermit jumped up and looked across the lake toward Bender Island where his mother was pointing. He couldn't believe it. Mrs. Bender was climbing onto her roof. She had one of her large straw hats on her head, and Kermit thought he could see her old cat, Titus, scrambling up beside her. She seemed to be pulling up the shingles and looking underneath.

"Good Lord!" exclaimed Mr. Fox.

"Oh dear," murmured Mrs. Fox, "I hope she doesn't fall."

2

The Stranger

Mrs. Bender did not fall. She must be a lot more athletic than she looks, Kermit thought, as he counted the worms he had dug the day before from one coffee can into another. They had watched the woman last night until she had given up prying under the shingles on her roof and had descended nimbly to the ground. Mrs. Fox had let out a sigh of relief, and Mr. Fox had gone into one of his frequent reveries on the wonders of the human race. Kermit himself had concluded that Mrs. Bender was probably a bit more peculiar than he had thought.

He dropped the last worm into the can and

wiped the dirt from his hands onto his khaki shorts. There were one hundred and fifty of them —a dollar and a half. Not bad for an afternoon's work, but still a far cry from the fifteen dollars he needed. He hoped that Brian had done better.

"Hi, Kermit!" Barbie waved enthusiastically from the garage as Kermit stopped his bike in front of the Digby bungalow.

"Hi, brat," Kermit replied with a grin. Though Barbie was an awful nuisance, Kermit couldn't help feeling flattered by the attention she paid him. She was sort of a cute kid with her stubby braids and freckles and she seemed to think Kermit was some kind of god on earth. "Brian around?"

Barbie pointed toward the back of the garage.

"Yeah, I'm here," Brian's disgusted voice came from behind the garage, "and I'll probably be here for the next week."

Kermit stepped around the building. "Cripes!" he exclaimed. "What's all that?"

Brian dropped his screw driver in disgust. It rolled to a stop against a mound of nuts and bolts. "This," said Brian, indicating the bits and pieces of machinery that surrounded him, "is my outboard motor and my father's electric drill and her"—he scowled at Barbie—"alarm clock."

"He's got them all mixed up and Mother says he has to stay right here until he has them all put back together again," Barbie volunteered. "I'm going to help."

Kermit looked at the mess. He couldn't think of anything to say that would cheer Brian up. There were an awful lot of screws and bolts. It looked like an all-day job—especially with Barbie helping.

"Aw, heck!" Brian kicked the alarm clock. "You going to Bigelow's?"

Kermit nodded.

"I've got a can of worms in the garage. You can take them, but there are only fifty." He gave his sister another dark look. "*She* was helping me again."

"I'll show you where they are, Kermit." Barbie took Kermit's hand and began pulling him around the side of the garage. Nothing seemed to bother her.

With a final sympathetic glance at Brian, Kermit let himself be dragged around the corner. "I'll come back tonight and we can hunt for night crawlers, O.K.?" he called over his shoulder.

Brian grunted his agreement.

It wasn't easy to get away from Barbie. First, she had to show him an old bird's nest she had found, and then a hunk of quartz someone had given her. The little pest wouldn't be half bad, Kermit thought, if she wasn't always tattling on Brian and messing around with his things.

Kermit put the can of worms in his basket and, waving good-by to Barbie, headed in the direction of Bigelow's General Store.

He could see that he was going to wind up doing most of the work in this worm business. Brian was always getting into some kind of trouble. But maybe that was just as well. When the time came, it would be hard for Brian not to loan him his share of the profits for Flash.

Flash! The very thought of him made Kermit pedal faster. How would it be to have Flash running beside him right now? That was one of the first things he would teach him. How to heel to a bicycle. He had read somewhere that dogs could be taught to do that. Then maybe he'd teach him . . .

But before Kermit could decide what the puppy's next lesson would be, he had arrived at Bigelow's. He set the kickstand of his bike and took the two cans of worms from the basket. If his hands hadn't been full, he would have pulled at his cowlick. Thinking about Flash worried him. Suppose no one wanted worms this summer. Suppose fishing had gone out of style and people were taking up water-skiing or something. He stepped through the open door and paused to let his eyes adjust to the change in light. Then he saw him.

A strange man was standing in front of the bulletin board. He was looking straight at the worm sign.

"Here's the boy you want," Mrs. Bigelow's voice came from behind the counter. "Kermit, this fellow here—Smith, is what he says his name is . . ." Mrs. Bigelow paused to show she had her doubts about that. "He wants to buy some worms."

The stranger turned around and peered at Kermit. Though his glasses were at least a quarter of an inch thick, he still seemed to squint, and one of his eyes twitched nervously at the corner. He didn't look like much of a sportsman. He was middle-aged and on the short side with a decidedly unathletic build. His skin was very pale. His clothes were all brand new, from his khaki hat, stuck with a dozen or more never-used fishing flies, to his stiff blue Levi's.

He was carrying a brand-new fishing pole rather gingerly in one hand, and around his neck hung a leather case. A camera, Kermit thought, or maybe binoculars. He looked exceedingly uncomfortable, and watching that eye twitch, Kermit began to feel uncomfortable too. He wished someone, even Mrs. Bigelow, would say something.

Finally, Mr. Smith cleared his throat and spoke. "So you are selling worms," he said, enunciating each word clearly, as though the language of fishermen was totally foreign.

Kermit nodded politely, though he thought that fact had already been established. Then, before they could begin another staring session, he said quickly, "How many do you want?"

The stranger's eye twitched violently for a second. "How many do you have?" he asked.

"Two hundred."

"I'll take them all." Mr. Smith's voice was suddenly decisive. He dug into his pocket for the money.

Kermit's mouth fell open. "You want all two hundred?" he asked.

The stranger nodded and handed him two dollar bills.

"Fish are gonna get mighty fat," Mrs. Bigelow

declared. She cast a hostile glance at Mr. Smith, then took a key from a nail on the wall and handed it to Kermit. "This gentleman's renting a boat too. How about getting the oars and showing him down to the boat dock? Strangers are apt to get lost around here."

Overwhelmed by his sudden good fortune, Kermit practically sailed out the door with the stranger close behind. Why, at this rate, he would have Flash in no time. He hoped Mr. Smith was planning on a long vacation. As he unlocked a pair of oars from the rack at the side of the store, his mind began clicking away like an adding machine. Suppose he bought two hundred worms a day. Two hundred into fifteen hundred—the numbers fell into place—that would be . . .

"Drat!"

A loud exclamation from the stranger interrupted Kermit's figuring. He hadn't locked his reel, and now he was hopelessly entangled in yards of fishing line. Kermit put down the oars and helped the man untangle himself. He's no fisherman, that's for sure, he thought as he unwound the line. A real greenhorn, that's what he is.

Still, as he picked up the oars once again and

headed across the road for the boat dock, Kermit
had the uneasy feeling that the stranger was not
as bumbling as he appeared. He felt that Mr.
Smith's eyes were glued right to the back of his

head, and he was glad when they reached the dock.

"I guess you can have whichever one you want," he said, setting down the oars.

The stranger looked the boats over and pointed to a green one tied at the end of the dock. "I'll take that one," he said.

Kermit placed the oars in the boat and pulled it in close. He held the rope taut while Mr. Smith stepped cautiously down from the dock. The boat rocked slightly. "Hold it still," cried the man. Kermit could see that he was really scared and tried to hold the rocking boat steady. With a thud, the man dropped down on the middle seat and started to fit the oars into the oarlocks.

Kermit pulled at his cowlick. "You're facing the wrong way," he pointed out. "Your back has to be to the bow of the boat."

The stranger looked bewildered, but after a moment he turned himself carefully around in the seat. He grabbed an oar just as it was slipping out of the oarlock.

Kermit handed down the two coffee cans full of worms. "Shall I push you off?" he asked.

The man mumbled something in reply as he

stowed the worms under the seat, and Kermit began to loosen the rope. As he leaned forward to give the boat a shove, Mr. Smith suddenly turned and looked directly at him. His nervous eye was surprisingly steady. "Is that Bender Island out there?" he asked.

"Yeah, that's it," Kermit replied.

The stranger's eye began to twitch again. He flushed slightly and mumbled something about the island being a pretty place.

"I guess it is," Kermit agreed as he shoved the boat away from the dock.

With a splash, the stranger thrust the oars into the water. After a few tries, he managed to get the boat moving toward the center of the lake. "Thanks," he called.

Kermit gave a half-hearted wave. He wasn't exactly eager to be friends with Mr. Smith, even if he had bought two hundred worms. Funny that he'd asked about Bender Island, he thought as he turned and walked back along the dock. Everyone seems to be interested in Mrs. Bender this summer.

Kermit wiped his brow with the back of his hand. He could feel the heat right through the rubber soles of his sneakers. Digging was the last thing he wanted to do on a day like this, but now that he'd sold all the worms, he had to get some more. Suppose another stranger like Mr. Smith came into Bigelow's and saw their sign.

He trudged slowly up the slope from the boat dock. Just as he reached the road, Kermit caught sight of Mrs. Carmichael, one of his mother's friends, coming out of Bigelow's with a huge over-loaded shopping bag in her arms. It looked like the bottom was breaking already. Kermit resisted an impulse to duck out of sight until the woman had passed. It wouldn't have done much good anyway. She had already seen him.

"Why, Kermit Fox! How nice to see you," she called, staggering slightly under her load. So naturally, Kermit had to offer to carry the groceries for her, and naturally, she accepted. It wasn't that Kermit had anything against Mrs. Carmichael. She was all right as his mother's friends went but, like all her friends, she talked too much. By the time he had set the bag down on her kitchen table, she had thanked him profusely and exclaimed at least ten times about how much he had grown since last summer. Kermit was so eager to get away that he turned down her offer of a plate of chocolate ice cream.

When he finally emerged from the Carmichael house, he could see by the sun that it was getting toward noon. It was a lot hotter too. A swim in the lake would feel awfully good, but he had wasted enough time already. He had to go back to Bigelow's, get his bike, and head home to start digging. He felt tired just thinking about it.

Mrs. Bigelow was out in front of the store polishing her gas pumps. She took great pride in the two pumps and kept them immaculately clean and shining. She caught sight of Kermit out of the corner of her eye. "Good thing you came back," she said, without stopping her polishing. "You got a job. And with none other than that crazy Mrs. Bender. She came by while you were gone. Said she had something for you to do out on her island. Said to send you right out there." Mrs. Bigelow spit on a stubborn spot and rubbed it with her cloth. "In a big hurry she was. Hopped right back into that leaky old boat of hers and rowed off. She's crazier than ever, I tell you, crazier than ever."

Kermit couldn't believe it. First a total stranger buying all his worms, and now old Mrs. Bender hiring him. It was too good to be true. Before

Mrs. Bigelow could start talking again, he jumped on his bike. "Thanks a lot for telling me," he said. "I'll go out there right away."

Mrs. Bigelow shook her head and went back to her polishing. She probably thinks I'm crazy, too, Kermit thought as he pedaled home. What kind of a job could Mrs. Bender want done? He remembered the woman poking around her roof the night before. Maybe she wants me to climb up there, he thought as he dumped his bike in the front yard and headed for the family rowboat. But that's all right. He gave the boat a shove and leaped expertly in—anything's better than digging.

He looked over his shoulder at the island and, for a moment, he couldn't help wondering—was Mrs. Bender really a little off? The big old house peeking out from the trees didn't look very inviting. Kermit rested his oars for a moment. What was it his father had said about *Mr.* Bender? That he'd been an amateur anthropologist? Or was it an archaeologist?

He looked at the island again, and suddenly his eyes opened wide. Rowing around the other side was Mr. Smith. As Kermit watched, he stopped rowing, took a pair of binoculars from the case around his neck, and peered intently at Mrs. Bender's house. The boat drifted slowly out of sight behind the trees. Kermit frowned. What could he be up to?

3

Bender Island

Kermit tied his boat to Mrs. Bender's sagging dock. The stranger had not appeared from behind the island. He probably stopped on the other side, Kermit decided as he climbed out of the boat. Not that there was anything wrong with that. He had a perfect right to fish off Bender Island. Even to look at it through binoculars, Kermit supposed.

He jumped to avoid a rotten board in the dock. Bender Island had seen better days. The stone steps leading from the boat dock to the house were falling this way and that. Two moss-covered Oriental lions ferociously guarded the front door, but the house drooped dejectedly with age. It was an enormous home, the sort people didn't build any more, especially on islands. Kermit's mother said that it had been in the Bender family for three generations. Looking at the peeling paint and falling shingles, Kermit didn't think it would last another three.

Maybe Mrs. Bender wants me to do some repair work, he thought as he ran up the steps to the house. He pounded the ornate medieval knocker against the front door. A little painting wouldn't be too hard.

"Who's there?" A muffled voice came from behind the door.

"It's me, Kermit Fox."

"Kermit Fox?" It was Mrs. Bender's voice all right, but it sounded like she had her head in a paper bag. "Oh yes. Come in."

Kermit pushed open the heavy door. "Golly," he murmured. The place looked like a tornado had hit it. Furniture was overturned, drawers were pulled open and their contents spilling out, and a pile of books lay in a heap beneath the empty bookcase. A couple of voodoo masks glowered unevenly from the walls and a tiger skin rug snarled wickedly from the floor. But where was Mrs. Bender? Kermit didn't see her anywhere.

"Mrs. Bender," he called hesitantly. "Where are you?"

A rustling sound came from the huge fireplace at one end of the room and a shower of cinders fell from the chimney.

Through the rain of ashes, Kermit could just make out two legs and the bottom of a skirt.

"Mrs. Bender," he called again.

"I'm in the chimney," Mrs. Bender replied. "Filthy place." More soot fell as she crawled out of the fireplace. "Achoo!" She gave a loud sneeze, shook the cinders from her skirt and flashed a dazzling smile at Kermit.

Her teeth, which would have been long and prominent under any circumstances, gleamed like piano keys in her soot-covered face. "Have a seat," she said, "while I wash up." And without a word of explanation, she swept away to the kitchen, casually removing a couple of Eskimo harpoons from her path and leaving a black trail of soot across the room.

Not quite believing what he had just seen, Kermit lowered himself into the nearest chair. It was a weird contraption made of zebra skins and elephant tusks. A warning *Hisss!* stopped him just

before he touched the seat. Mrs. Bender's huge
orange cat, Titus, glared at him from the chair.
Kermit backed away and lowered himself onto the
overstuffed sofa. He sat on the edge, keeping a
nervous eye on Titus. The old cat continued to
stare without blinking an eye.

"Good of you to come so promptly," Mrs.

Bender called from the kitchen. "I have a most important job for you."

Kermit hoped it wasn't cleaning the chimney. His father had read him a book called *Oliver Twist* about a boy who swept chimneys and it didn't sound like much fun. He took his eyes off Titus for a moment and looked around the room. The house was weird enough at any time, but in its present disorder it seemed even more bizarre. He wondered if Mrs. Bender could be moving. But there were no packing crates to be seen. And she certainly wasn't house cleaning. Not with that trail of soot she had left across the floor.

"Titus, you old devil, are you giving Kermit a hard time?" Mrs. Bender strode briskly across the room and swept the cat off the chair. "He's a nasty old thing, but pay him no mind," she said with another of her toothy smiles.

Kermit managed a smile, but he couldn't help staring at Mrs. Bender. Her gray hair was done up in an enormous braid wrapped around her head, and a heavy—rather sooty—shell necklace dangled from her neck. Her skirt and blouse were embroidered with some kind of Indian design. Kermit guessed she was old enough to be a grandmother, but she certainly didn't look like one.

"I suppose you are wondering what I want you to do," she said. "I suppose you are wondering what all this"—she took in the room with a sweep of her hand—"is about."

Kermit nodded, but Mrs. Bender didn't seem to notice. She paced back and forth in the only clear space in the room and twirled the shells on her necklace until Kermit began to feel almost hypnotized. Finally she stopped in front of him, her hands on her hips. "But I am afraid that you must remain in the dark, as they say. For the time being at any rate."

Kermit fought back an urge to pull at his cowlick, and tried to look as though he understood.

"No," Mrs. Bender said, resuming her pacing. "It is all very *hush-hush*. Something like this in the wrong hands would be disastrous. A blow to the fund of human knowledge. A . . ." She paused and smiled slightly at the bewildered expression on Kermit's face. "Well, that's enough. You get the picture, I'm sure. Now, if you'll just follow me." She turned away and swept toward a door at the end of the room.

Completely confused, Kermit followed her through the narrow doorway. "Yikes!" he cried. He grabbed at the wall to keep his balance. They were standing at the top of the stairs leading to the cellar. Kermit had almost stepped off the edge.

Mrs. Bender flicked on the light switch. The dingy rock walls and hard dirt floor below were bathed in an eerie glow. Kermit thought it looked more like a dungeon than a cellar. Mrs. Bender took a brand-new shovel from a nail on the landing wall and handed it to him.

"This is the job I hired you for," she said. "All I want you to do is dig. Start anywhere you like. You don't have to go deep—a foot will be sufficient."

Kermit looked at Mrs. Bender, then at the shovel in his hand, then back at Mrs. Bender. He could not believe his ears. Did she really want him to dig up the cellar floor? A foot deep?

Mrs. Bender gave him a sly wink and put a finger to her lips. "Remember, all very *hush-hush*," she whispered. And before Kermit could say a word, she slipped out the door.

He didn't know how he got down the steps, but the next thing he knew he was standing on the dirt floor looking up into Titus's big green eyes. The cat had stationed himself sphinx-like on the steps to observe the proceedings.

Kermit turned the shovel over in his hands. The price sticker from Bigelow's General Store was still on the handle. Now he knew why Mrs. Bender had bought it. He stuck the point into the close-packed earth and pushed. With a sigh, he turned over a shovelful of dirt. Digging! What a job!

He looked dismally at the expanse of hard-packed earth before him and dug in again. He felt tired already. What was Mrs. Bender planning to do? Plant mushrooms? He couldn't even begin to guess what all that *"hush-hush"* talk had been about.

"Cripes! How can I work with you here?" Kermit pushed Titus out of the way with the shovel. The old cat had tired of watching from the stairs and had come down to help. He was stalking something in Kermit's shovelful of dirt.

"Scram, I said." Kermit stamped his foot at the big cat, and something pink slithered quickly away in the overturned earth.

"Worms!" Kermit looked at the earth he had already overturned and saw that it was full of them. The cellar was a regular paradise for worms. He grabbed a few and looked around for something to put them in. But except for a few battered wooden crates standing by the door that led outside, the cellar seemed to be completely empty.

"Wouldn't you know it," he muttered. If he could collect a few worms, the job might not be so bad. But he couldn't just stuff them into his pockets. Then he noticed an old flowerpot. It was sitting on the sill of a small window recessed in the very top of the cellar wall.

Kermit dragged one of the crates beneath the window and climbed up. He looked out through the dusty glass and got a worm's-eye view of the island, for the window was only a foot high and on a level with the ground. It looked quiet and peaceful outside. A daddy longlegs was making its way over the long grass blades in front of the window. Kermit watched as it wavered atop a blade, thrusting its legs around for something to grab on to. It had almost reached a slender twig when all of a sudden a gigantic foot in a blue canvas shoe came into view at the top of the window. It crashed mercilessly down, followed closely by its mate.

Kermit winced as though he'd been stepped on himself. The crate he was standing on wobbled dangerously and he felt himself falling. He hit the ground with a thud. An ear-piercing shriek

arose from beneath him. Screaming like a banshee, Titus struggled to get out from beneath Kermit who had landed smack on his tail.

"What in the world is going on?" cried Mrs. Bender, appearing at the head of the stairs. "Titus!" She raced down the steps and rescued the screaming cat. "Kermit, what are you doing to poor Titus?"

"I . . . he . . . that is . . ." Kermit stammered.

"Well?" demanded Mrs. Bender, looking narrowly at him. "Why were you sitting on Titus's tail?"

"I wasn't sitting on his tail," Kermit protested. "I mean, I was—but not on purpose. I fell. I saw a man. I mean, a man's foot. Or feet. Through that window."

Mrs. Bender let Titus drop to the floor. "This is terrible!" she exclaimed. She grabbed Kermit by the hand and pulled him up from the ground. "Hurry," she called as she flew up the stairs and out the front door. "Search the bushes, search everywhere!" she directed, plunging into the evergreens. "It's him, that unprincipled cad. This is just what I was afraid of."

Kermit raced around the side of the house and

located the cellar window. The grass was thick, so there were no footprints—not that Kermit would have known what to do with a footprint if he had found one. Then he noticed something small and brightly colored clinging to a tall weed. A fishing fly! He picked the tiny feathered fly off the weed and tugged hard at his cowlick.

"Nothing on that side," Mrs. Bender called. "Anything here?" She came breathlessly around the corner of the house. Kermit quickly shoved the fly into his pocket.

"Nothing here either," Kermit said, crossing his fingers behind his back.

"Well, I guess that's that," the woman declared. She looked tired and worried. "You had better go home, Kermit. You've done enough work for today. Come back tomorrow, please." She ran her hand wearily over her eyes.

Kermit hesitated. If Mrs. Bender was in some kind of trouble, he didn't think he should leave her alone. But she motioned him away with a wave of her hand. "Don't worry, I'll be all right," she said, attempting a smile. "Just come back tomorrow."

Mumbling a hasty good-by, Kermit turned and ran for his boat. A few drops of rain began to fall as he thrust the oars into the water and struck out for home. By the time he reached the Fox's boat dock, what had started out as a gentle afternoon shower had turned into a downpour. Kermit was soaked to the skin, but he hardly noticed. He had more important things on his mind than rain.

4
Free Puppies

Why, Kermit, you're sopping wet. Have you been out on the lake in this rain?"

"Aw, Mom!" Kermit stood in the middle of the kitchen, a puddle of water growing slowly around his feet. "It doesn't hurt to get a little wet," he protested. But Mrs. Fox made him change into dry clothes and sit by the heater for half an hour anyway. Kermit extracted the fly from the pocket of his wet shorts and held it by the heater to dry. The man who had walked by Mrs. Bender's cellar window must have been Smith. This was one of those brand-new flies he had stuck in his hat. But why had he been prowling around the island? And why had Mrs. Bender been so upset? Kermit couldn't figure it out. By dinnertime, the scalp under his cowlick was sore from so much pulling.

"You really must stop that habit," Mrs. Fox said. "It's very distracting to talk to someone who keeps pulling away at his head. Soon you'll have me doing it."

"Or me," added Kermit's father, pulling at the few precious strands of hair on his balding head. "And that would be disastrous."

"I'll try," Kermit promised. Luckily, there was fried chicken for dinner and that took two hands. Kermit made an effort to pay attention to what his parents were saying. Sometimes they said very interesting things, and he had learned a lot from dinner-table conversations. But tonight, he just couldn't concentrate. His mind kept wandering to Mrs. Bender or to the little red and yellow fly in his pocket. He hardly noticed that dessert was peach cobbler, one of his favorites.

"Kermit, where are you tonight?" his mother said. "I've asked you twice if you want some more cobbler."

"Oh. Yes, Mom." Kermit passed his plate. "I was just thinking of something else."

"These peaches are the first of the season," Mrs. Fox said as she spooned another helping onto Kermit's plate. "I went to Manley's Peach Farm today." She winked at Kermit's father. "It's a very interesting place," she said, passing the plate back to Kermit.

Kermit's father smiled and put on the mysterious look he wore around Christmas and Kermit's birthday. "I should say it's interesting. Do you know what Mr. Manley has in his barn, Kermit?"

Wondering what was going on, Kermit shook his head.

"A litter of puppies," Mr. Fox said dramatically.

Kermit felt a sudden twinge in his stomach.

"He is trying to find homes for them," Kermit's mother added. "What do you think of that?"

Kermit swallowed hard and, luckily, a piece of peach cobbler stuck in his throat. He coughed so violently that he had to run to the kitchen for a glass of water.

Puppies! Kermit gulped the water down and gasped for breath. A litter of free puppies, and his parents were planning to get him one.

"Kermit, are you all right?" Mrs. Fox called.

Kermit had to think fast. He couldn't go back

to the table—not while they still had puppies on their minds. "I'm O.K.," he called. "But I just remembered, I've got to go to Brian's."

"But don't you want . . ."

Kermit was out the door before his mother could say another word. He jumped on his bike and pedaled toward the Digby bungalow. His parents were just too nice, that was the problem. Suppose they went out and got one of those puppies as a surprise? What if it was there in the front yard when he woke up tomorrow morning? Of course, he could tell them about Flash, but he didn't think that would do any good. With a whole litter of free puppies available, they would never let him spend fifty dollars on a dog.

There was only one thing he could do. Get the money for Flash before they got him one of those puppies. By the time he reached Brian's house, Kermit had convinced himself that he could do it. He would hunt night crawlers all night and dig worms all day if need be. Nothing would come between him and Flash.

Brian was in the garage. "I've got the outboard motor all done," he announced when he saw Kermit. "Do you see anything around here that looks like the mainspring of an alarm clock?" He began to rummage through the pile of metal pieces on the garage floor.

But Kermit didn't care about alarm clocks. He cared about worms. "Come on. Let's hunt night crawlers," he said.

"But they don't come up until dark," Brian pointed out. "What's the hurry?"

"I need that money fast," Kermit replied. Then he told Brian about his parents and the free puppies.

"Boy, I'd sure like to have one," Brian murmured. "I could too, if it wasn't for her."

Kermit didn't have to ask who he was talking about. Barbie was afraid of dogs. She screamed her head off whenever she saw one. "Well, I don't want one of Mr. Manley's puppies," Kermit said quickly, before he could start feeling sorry for Brian. "I want Flash, so that's why we've got to get lots of worms tonight." He looked out the garage door. It was almost dark.

"There are some flashlights around here somewhere," Brian said, poking around in a pile of old cartons. "I hid them from Barbie. Aha!" He dug two flashlights out of a box of old paint rags and handed one to Kermit. They found a couple of coffee cans and switched on their lights.

"Careful," Kermit whispered as they stepped off the driveway, "we don't want to scare them."

"There's one!" Brian exclaimed, shining his light on the ground. He made a dive for a long pink shape lying on the wet leaves, but he wasn't quick enough. The worm slithered into its hole, leaving Brian with nothing but a trail of slime on his hand. Brian wiped his fingers on his pants in disgust. Kermit sympathized with him. That was the one thing he didn't like about hunting night crawlers.

For a while they worked quietly, with only an occasional cry of "I got one" to break the silence. The worms were lying all over the ground, but they were alert. At the slightest vibration, they slipped away into the earth. Kermit kicked angrily at the hole where an unusually big one had just disappeared.

"Aw, let's knock off for a while," Brian groaned. He pulled some gum from his pocket and handed a stick to Kermit. Kermit bit into it gratefully. That was one of the good things about having Brian for a friend. His mother didn't care what he ate. He could chew all the gum and drink all the Cokes he wanted. He could even eat those wax candies in the shape of soda bottles right in front of his mother, and she never said a word.

"I saw you out on the lake today," Brian said after they had chewed for a while. "Where were you going?"

Kermit almost swallowed his gum. Mrs. Bender! He had been so busy thinking about Flash that he had forgotten about his trip to the island. Now, he began to tell Brian about his strange job, and the even stranger Mr. Smith. Of course, Mrs. Bender had said that it was all very "hush-hush," but Kermit didn't see any harm in telling Brian. They always shared their secrets. As they sat in the darkness talking, their eyes wandered across the lake to the dim outline of Bender Island.

Suddenly, Brian jumped up. "Hey, look at that," he cried, pointing toward the island.

"Look at what?" Kermit peered into the darkness. He didn't see anything.

"There it is again," Brian said.

This time Kermit did see. A light appeared on the island, then went out. In another moment it appeared again, a little farther over. Wordlessly, the boys watched. The light went out for a longer time—two or three minutes at least. Then it reappeared.

"It's someone walking around out there with a flashlight," Kermit said. "It must be Mrs. Bender . . . or . . ." He let his voice trail off. Could it be Mr. Smith?

The light went out again, and the boys raced down to the Digby's boat dock where they could get a better view of the island.

"What could . . ." Brian began in a whisper, but before he could finish, there was a loud splash

in the water. Waves lapped against the dock posts and a water-choked voice cried, "Help! I can't swim."

Brian dived for the Digby rowboat and pulled an oar from its lock. "Take this," he called, holding out the oar to the thrashing, sputtering form in the water. The oar was grabbed with a jerk that almost pulled him off the dock. He regained his balance and, with Kermit's help, dragged the oar and its passenger close to the dock. A hand reached blindly up. Pulling with all their might, Kermit and Brian dragged the man from the water. He lay on his stomach gasping for breath, his feet still dangling in the lake.

"Get the rest of him up," Brian directed.

Kermit grabbed the man's legs and pulled them from the water. Taking the feet around the ankles, he swung them heavily onto the dock. All at once, he jumped back as though he'd been bitten. The man's feet fell with a thud and Kermit stared wordlessly at the blue canvas shoes.

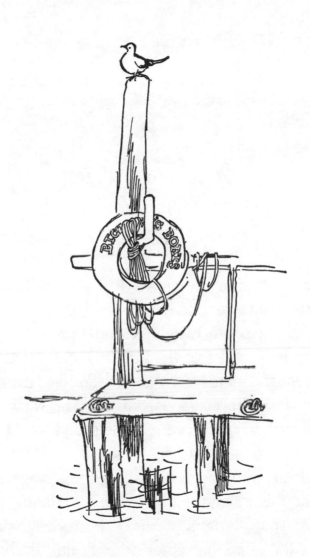

5

Mr. Smith Again

The man struggled slowly to his feet. Breathing heavily, he stared at Kermit for a moment. Then his eye began to twitch. Kermit shoved his hand into the pocket that held the red and yellow fishing fly and stared back at Mr. Smith. It was the only thing he could do. He was sure·that if he had tried to speak, not a single sound would have come from his throat.

Brian, who had been fishing the stranger's hat from the water, finally broke the staring spell. "Are you all right, mister?" he asked, handing him the khaki hat stuck with fishing flies. "Do you want to come up to the house and dry off?"

The man took the hat from Brian. "No, I'm

all right," he said quickly. "If I could just get my boat . . ."

The words were no sooner out of his mouth, than Kermit made a grab for the rented boat floating at the side of the dock. The sooner Mr. Smith was gone, the better. The stranger seemed to feel the same way. He scrambled off the dock and into the boat.

"But shouldn't you dry off?" Brian protested. "What's wrong with you, Foxie? Can't you see . . ." He let the words trail off. Kermit had shot him a look that could have withered an oak tree.

The stranger seemed relieved. He grasped his oars and thrust them awkwardly into the water. "I'll just be on my way," he mumbled as the boat moved away from the dock. "Thank you for the help."

"What's up?" Brian whispered when the stranger was gone. "Why are you acting so funny?"

"That," Kermit replied gravely, "was Mr. Smith."

"You mean . . ."

Kermit nodded. "None other. Now I'm sure he was the one prowling around Mrs. Bender's. Did you see his shoes?"

Brian hadn't.

"Well, they were just like the ones I saw from the cellar window," Kermit explained. "Blue canvas with ripple soles. Brand new."

Brian looked impressed at his friend's powers of observation.

"I'll bet he was poking around the island and Mrs. Bender heard him. That's why she's out there with her flashlight," Kermit thought out loud. "I'd sure like to know what's going on."

"Maybe we'd better tell Sergeant Toohill," Brian said seriously. "He could be dangerous." He started up the slope at a run, and was halfway to the house before Kermit could grab his shirt-tail and stop him.

"Are you nuts?" he exclaimed. "Tell Sergeant Toohill and give him something more to tease us about?"

"But this is different," Brian protested.

"No," Kermit said firmly. "This time we're not telling the sergeant a thing until we've got proof. Real proof, not just shoes and fishing flies."

"But how . . ."

"We'll go out to the island tomorrow and investigate," Kermit replied calmly. The idea had come to him all at once. Kermit Fox, private investigator. He liked the way it sounded. But Brian looked skeptical.

"Just think of it. Suppose this Smith is some kind of thief or . . ." Kermit stopped. "That's it! Smith *is* a thief."

"Aw, come on," Brian objected. "Mrs. Bender doesn't have anything worth stealing."

"She might. Look, I told you what a mess the house was in and how she had me digging up the cellar. Now, couldn't she be looking for something? Something valuable. Buried treasure, even."

Kermit's eyes lit up. Maybe *he* was digging for buried treasure. He could imagine his shovel striking something hard. He would pull a rusty old chest out of the ground, break open the hasp, and dig his hands into . . .

"Rats!"

"Huh?" Kermit came out of his dream.

Brian pointed toward the house. Barbie was stepping out the door. "I'm going to help you, Brian," she called. "Mother says I can."

Brian groaned, and Kermit quickly decided it was time to go home. "Tomorrow, then?" he whispered, just as Barbie joined them. Brian gave a quick nod, and before his sister could ask any questions, he dangled a fat night crawler in front of her nose. Kermit could still hear her screaming when he was on his bike and halfway home.

Private eye. Secret agent Fox. He turned the titles over in his mind and decided they sounded good. Suppose there was a fortune hidden on Bender Island, and he, Kermit Fox—with the help, of course, of his faithful friend Brian Digby— saved it from the clutches of the mysterious Mr. Smith. That would give Sergeant Toohill something to talk about. And who could tell, there might even be a reward—say, fifteen dollars or so.

It was a happy thought to fall asleep on, but by the next morning, Kermit was beginning to have some serious doubts. After all, Mr. Smith *could* be dangerous. He looked sort of meek, but Kermit had seen enough movies to know that didn't mean anything. That type often turned out to be the toughest of all.

He dressed slowly and spent an unusually long time brushing his teeth. Maybe going to the island was not such a good idea after all.

"Brian's here," Mrs. Fox called.

Kermit shoved his feet into his sneakers and ambled into the kitchen. Brian was having a second breakfast. A two-pound-size coffee can sat before him on the table.

"The night crawlers," Brian mumbled between bites of toast.

"That's just what I suspected." Kermit's mother took the can and carried it gingerly to the back stoop. "They'll be quite happy out there," she said, setting a glass of milk and a plate of scrambled eggs in front of Kermit.

"I thought we could take them by Bigelow's before . . ." Brian's voice trailed off, and he raised his eyebrows significantly.

Kermit took a gulp of milk and glanced quickly at his friend. If Brian wasn't going to chicken out, he couldn't either. He suddenly remembered that he'd promised Mrs. Bender he'd be back today, anyway. Still, it wouldn't hurt to waste a little time around Bigelow's General Store. They might even find out something about Mr. Smith. He wolfed down his eggs and finished his milk in two swallows. "Let's get started," he said, trying to put some confidence into his voice.

"But, Kermit . . ." Mrs. Fox pointed to the slice of toast and jelly she had just put at her son's place.

"I'll take it for him, Mrs. Fox," Brian offered,

and snatched the toast as he followed Kermit out the door. They hopped on their bikes, Kermit balancing the worm can in his basket, and started down the road. "What are we going to do when we get there?" Brian asked when he had finished the last bite of Kermit's toast and jelly.

Kermit looked grim and made no reply. How should he know what they would do? He'd never caught a thief before. Good old Brian hadn't stared into Mr. Smith's twitching eye like he had. He thought it was all a game.

Brian swallowed. "You don't think he's . . . uh . . . dangerous or something, do you?" he asked hesitantly.

Kermit frowned. "Maybe," he replied darkly. Out of the corner of his eye he could see Brian gulp, and then Bigelow's General Store came into view.

"Maybe she's got a new shipment of comics," Brian said, looking hopefully at his friend.

Kermit took up this new suggestion immediately. He was glad to see that Brian was no longer so eager to go to the island. "Yeah, maybe she does," he said as they propped their bikes up, took the can of worms, and stepped inside. A quick look around told them there was no one in the store but Mrs. Bigelow and, luckily, she was in no mood for conversation. She was deeply absorbed in the obituary column of *The Poughkeepsie New Yorker*, and hardly noticed when Kermit put the can of worms behind the counter.

Brian was already standing at the magazine rack with his nose in a *Batman* comic. Kermit knew it was one he'd read at least ten times. He picked out a well-worn *Superman* and sat down on a pile of *Ladies' Home Journals*. It didn't take long to get through Mrs. Bigelow's meager selection of comics. Kermit wondered if she ever sold any. Everyone he knew read them for free, and by the time the next month's shipment came in, they were pretty dog-eared.

Brian put down his comic and wandered over to the case of jackknives. Kermit followed, and they wasted some more time looking at the knives. They never seemed to change either. Then they moved to the fishing reels, and finally, as a last resort, to the piles of striped T shirts and dungarees. Kermit could see that they weren't going to be able to waste much more time. After they'd gone over the dungarees twice, he cleared his throat. "Guess we'd better get going," he said.

"Uh . . . yeah," Brian mumbled. "Guess so."

Taking one last look at the jackknives, they moved reluctantly toward the door.

Just as they stepped outside, the Foxes' old station wagon pulled up in front of Mrs. Bigelow's shiny gas pumps. Kermit's father leaned across the front seat. "How'd you boys like to go to Manley's Peach Farm?" he called.

In a flash, Kermit and Brian were in the back seat and Mr. Fox was turning the car back onto the road. Kermit took a deep breath. What luck! They might spend the rest of the morning at the farm. He shot a quick glance at Brian, who looked equally relieved.

"I thought you'd want to go to the peach farm after what we told you last night." Mr. Fox gave Kermit a mysterious smile through the rearview mirror.

After last night? Oh no! Kermit sank down in the seat. How could he have forgotten? The litter of free puppies was at Manley's Peach Farm. He stole a glance in the mirror. His father was smiling happily and humming a little tune. Kermit sank down farther and closed his eyes.

When they stopped at the fruit stand in front of the farm, he had to force himself to get out of the car. His father kept giving him mysterious

smiles. When Mr. Manley came out of the stand, he drew him aside and began to talk in a low voice. Kermit hung around the car while his father bought a couple of pounds of peaches. That was just part of the game, because Kermit knew his mother had a whole bushel of them in the kitchen at this very moment. Suddenly he felt that peaches—even made into peach cobbler— were no longer his favorite fruit.

Kermit's father winked at Mr. Manley, and the farmer grinned broadly. "Say, boys, I've got something out in the barn I'll bet you'd like to see," he said, returning Mr. Fox's wink.

Kermit was about to say he didn't feel like seeing anything just now—that he felt faint maybe or sick to his stomach—when good old Brian piped up, "What is it?"

Kermit scowled fiercely, but Brian didn't even notice. He was already following Mr. Manley toward the barn.

"This is something we don't want to miss," Kermit's father said with a smile. He put his hand on Kermit's shoulder and started after Brian and the farmer. Kermit's feet felt as if they were stuck in concrete, but he had to walk toward the barn.

They found Mr. Manley and Brian already kneeling down beside an old calf pen.

"Gosh, Kermit. Look!" Brian exclaimed. "Aren't they something?"

Kermit looked, and suddenly he felt as if he might really be sick. Tumbling around in the straw were five furry little puppies. They were fat and cute, but compared to Flash . . . The picture Kermit had of himself with the golden boxer at his side leaped into his mind. He could feel those dark, intelligent eyes looking at him, that silky muzzle pushing against his hand. No. He could never be satisfied with one of these puppies—not after knowing Flash.

"When will they be ready to leave their mother?" Kermit heard his father ask. He held his breath, as the farmer replied, "Oh, I'd say about as long as it would take a boy to buy a collar and leash, fix up a place for one to stay, and get back here. Just about that long, I'd say."

Kermit looked at the penful of puppies and his heart sank straight down to his toes.

"Did you hear that, Kermit?" said his father, smiling. "Think we might come back tomorrow?"

Tomorrow! Could he possibly get Flash before then? It looked hopeless, but he would have to try. Meanwhile, his father would be suspicious if he didn't show a little enthusiasm. He picked up the nearest puppy and scratched it behind the ears. "Sure, Dad. That would be great."

Brian looked at him in astonishment. "How about . . ." he began, but Kermit silenced him with a terrible scowl. He looked down at the fat puppy in his lap. Now he really had problems. Almost fifteen dollars in just one day. Could it be done?

6
Buried Treasure

Here's some money for ice cream," Mr. Fox said when he left them in front of Bigelow's. He tousled Kermit's hair. "Don't spend it all on comic books."

Kermit wished his father weren't being so nice. It made him feel guilty about keeping Flash a secret, but if he did manage to get the puppy, he was sure they would understand. No one could possibly resist Flash.

Kermit had too much on his mind to think about food, but Brian ordered two fudge ripple ice-cream cones with chocolate sprinkles from Mrs. Bigelow. "If you're going to get fifteen bucks by tomorrow," he told Kermit, "you'll need plenty of strength."

Mrs. Bigelow put down her newspaper and scooped the ice cream out of the freezer. "If you want to earn some money," she said, handing them the cones, "I'll give you fifty cents to take these groceries out to Mrs. Bender. She ordered them yesterday and that no-good delivery boy of mine's gone fishing."

Kermit gulped. He had managed to put Mrs. Bender out of his mind, and could easily have forgotten entirely about the trip to Bender Island. But fifty cents was fifty cents. "I guess we could," he said. "We were going out there anyway, weren't we, Brian?"

"Yeah," Brian admitted. "I guess we were." He picked up one box of groceries, carefully balancing his ice-cream cone, while Kermit took the other and pocketed the fifty cents.

"Take one of my boats," Mrs. Bigelow said, handing Kermit the key. "And, oh yes, I almost forgot. Mrs. Sprague was in here today and saw your worm sign. She wants five hundred by tomorrow."

"Five hundred!" Kermit nearly dropped his box of groceries.

Mrs. Bigelow nodded. "That's what I said. The Home Bureau's having their annual picnic at the lake tomorrow and Mrs. Sprague thought they might like to do some fishing. There are forty ladies, so I said five hundred would probably do nicely."

Brian groaned. "That's an awful lot of worms."

"That's what you have to expect when you're in business," Mrs. Bigelow replied. "You advertise, you gotta produce."

"We'll have them here tomorrow morning," Kermit promised.

"Nice big ones, now," Mrs. Bigelow called after them as they went out the door. "That's what I told her to expect."

"Cripes!" Brian exclaimed in disgust as he set his box of groceries in the boat. "We'll never be able to dig that many by tomorrow."

"We've got to," Kermit replied, feeling better already. He had gulped down his ice-cream cone and taken a pair of oars from the rack. He fitted them hastily into the oarlocks. "You heard what my father said about those free puppies. We can't afford to pass up five bucks. I've only got until tomorrow."

"Guess you're planning on borrowing my share, eh Foxie," Brian grumbled.

"Fox . . ." Kermit began, but he stopped himself just in time. He couldn't afford to have a fight with Brian, not when he needed his share of the worm money. He pulled hard on the oars and headed the boat for the island. Maybe he'd do the rowing on the way home too. He started adding in his head. He had five dollars, and then the two dollars from Mr. Smith, and five dollars from the Home Bureau tomorrow. And the fifty cents in his pocket right now. That would make twelve dollars and fifty cents. Maybe Mr. Taylor would settle for that if he explained how important it was.

"Do you really think she's got some kind of treasure hidden out there?" Brian asked after a while. He had finished his ice-cream cone, savoring it down to the last crumb, and seemed to be in a better mood.

Kermit glanced at Bender Island and shrugged his shoulders. In the light of day, the treasure idea sounded a little farfetched. "Well, maybe it's not treasure," he said, "but she's looking for something and so is that Smith guy."

Brian looked thoughtfully at the island ahead

of them. "*Mr.* Bender sure collected a lot of junk," he mused. "I wonder what kind of a guy he was."

Kermit suddenly stopped rowing. "Brian, that's it!" he exclaimed. Why hadn't he thought of it before? He remembered the newspaper article his father had been reading the night they saw Mrs. Bender climbing on her roof. "He was an amateur archaeologist, or maybe it was an anthropologist," he said excitedly.

Brian shrugged his shoulders. "So?"

"So, archaeologists look for old things, don't they?" Kermit explained, "and old things are valuable. At least, sometimes they are."

"I get it," Brian said, and his voice began to sound excited too. "You think that some of that junk of his is valuable. Maybe those crazy statues are worth a fortune."

Kermit pulled at his cowlick. "Well, not the statues," he said slowly. "Because whatever it is, it's hidden. Not even *Mrs.* Bender knows where it is."

"Gosh!" Brian's eyes lit up. "It could be anything. Gold doubloons, even."

Kermit tugged harder at his carrot-colored hair. He was trying to remember what else the article had said about Mr. Bender. There was some-

thing about the Orient, but then they had seen
Mrs. Bender on the roof, and his father had
never finished. He started rowing again, throwing
all his strength into the oars and making the boat
move quickly through the water. If there really
were gold doubloons and they found them, Mrs.
Bender would be sure to give them a reward.

He turned and saw that Bender Island was already looming large in front of them. He noticed, as he had before, how badly the house needed repairs and felt a twinge of guilt for thinking about a reward. Poor old Mrs. Bender would probably need the whole treasure for herself.

"Hey, watch out!" Kermit was thinking so hard that he almost rowed straight into the dock. Brian's yell stopped him just in time. Good thing, too, he thought as he rested his oars. The whole thing would probably have collapsed. Brian jumped out and tied the boat to a post. They lifted out the boxes of groceries.

"Gosh!" said Brian looking up at the house and the thick undergrowth on the island. "It could take years to find anything hidden around this place."

Kermit had to admit that Brian was right, but there was no point in getting discouraged before they even began. "Come on," he said, starting up the stone steps. "We've got to deliver these groceries anyway."

The boxes were heavy and by the time they reached the top, both boys were breathing hard. Kermit balanced his box of groceries on one knee and rapped on the door. There was a sound of hurried footsteps, and then the door was opened just a crack.

"Who's there?" a voice asked suspiciously.

"Kermit Fox, Mrs. Bender," Kermit replied.

"Oh!" the woman sounded relieved. "Come in." She slid the chain off the door and opened it wide. "I was beginning to wonder if you were going to come back," she said with a toothy smile. "And you've brought my groceries too. How very nice. If you'll just set them in the kitchen . . ."

Kermit noticed that the room had been put back in order. The books were in the bookcase, chairs were turned right side up, the cinders had been swept from the hearth, and the tiger skin rug brushed clean. Evidently, Mrs. Bender had finished searching the living room.

"Do you remember my friend Brian Digby?" Kermit asked when they had put the groceries in the kitchen.

Mrs. Bender squinted at Brian and moved a step closer. Brian squirmed under her intent gaze. "Why, of course," she said at last. "The boy who likes cookies."

Brian's cheeks turned bright red.

"Isn't that right?" Mrs. Bender inquired. "I seem to remember . . ."

"Yeah, that's right," Brian said quickly, before

she could elaborate on how many he had eaten one day last summer.

"I'm sorry I don't have any now," Mrs. Bender murmured, more to herself than to the boys, "but I've been so busy . . ." She twirled her apricot pit necklace distractedly.

Kermit glanced at Brian. He knew this was the time to bring up Mr. Smith and find out what was going on, but somehow, he couldn't think of the right way to put it. He didn't want to seem too nosy. After all, Mrs. Bender had said it was all very *"hush-hush."* Still, how could they help her if they didn't even know what she was looking for? He pulled on his cowlick. "Uh . . . we were wondering . . ." he began.

"Wondering?" Mrs. Bender stopped twirling the apricot pits. "Oh, you must excuse me. I was thinking of something else." She looked from Kermit to Brian and snapped her fingers. "Why, there are two of you!" she exclaimed. "That's perfect. The cellar will take only half as long. If Brian would like a job too, that is."

Brian gulped. "Well . . . uh . . . sure, I guess so," he stammered. "Only we'd sort of like to know . . ."

"That's fine," declared Mrs. Bender rubbing

her hands together and paying no attention to what Brian was trying to say. "Oh, we won't let that conniving scoundrel get his hands on them." She paced rapidly back and forth. "We won't . . . but why am I wasting time? There's work to be done." She herded the astonished boys toward the cellar door. "You can use that spade," she told Brian, pointing to a battered tool hanging on the wall of the cellar landing. "I'm going out to the end of the island. If you find anything . . . unusual . . . come and get me at once."

"But . . ." Kermit began, then stopped, for he saw it was useless. Mrs. Bender had already plopped one of her huge straw hats on her head, taken a pair of pruning shears from the kitchen table, and with a final toothy smile, exited out the front door.

"Boy," Brian said in amazement. "I think she really is batty, just like Mrs. Bigelow says."

"And we still don't know what we're looking for," Kermit said, switching on the cellar light.

Brian started down the stairs. "Digging," he groaned. "What a crummy job."

Kermit couldn't have agreed more. He picked up his shovel from the ground where he'd dropped it the day before and dug it into the dirt. Then he remembered the worms in the cellar and brightened a little. Maybe they could get two jobs done at once. The flowerpot was still on the window sill, and he climbed up on the crate and brought it safely down. Brian plugged up the hole with a wad of chewing gum, and they dumped in some earth.

Kermit counted each worm they dropped into the pot and, as the number mounted, his hopes rose. He just might get Flash after all. "Hey, what's he up to?" Brian asked when they had been digging for a while. He leaned on his spade and pointed toward the cellar door which led outside.

Mrs. Bender's old cat had followed them down the cellar and was sniffing suspiciously along the bottom of the door. "Who knows?" Kermit replied as he picked up his shovel and moved to the far corner of the cellar. "I'm going to dig over here for a while." Something about the corner struck him as more promising. He dug his shovel in and turned over a pile of earth.

Brian wiped his brow and watched him. Titus gave a loud, insistent meow. "Maybe he wants to go out," Brian suggested.

"Aw, he can go up the stairs and out the kitchen door," Kermit grumbled.

Titus meowed again. "Well, I'm going to let him out here," Brian said. "We could use some air anyway." He shoved the door open. Titus streaked out into the sunlight. Brian took a deep breath. "Sure is a nice day for swimming," he said. "I wish . . ."

"Brian!" Kermit interrupted. "Come here!"

While Brian had been talking, Kermit had been digging, and all at once his shovel had struck something hard. "I found something!" he exclaimed. Brian was at his side in a second. There was a square metal box buried in the dirt. "This must be it," Kermit said in a whisper.

"The treasure!" Brian peered over his shoulder. "Well, pull it out," he urged.

Kermit tugged at the handle attached to the top and slowly the box came free of the surrounding earth. "Gosh, it weighs a ton." He dragged the box out of the hole. There was no lock, but the hasp had rusted. Kermit took out his pocketknife and pried it free from the staple.

"Open it!" Brian pounded on Kermit's shoulder in excitement.

Kermit half closed his eyes. Visions of gold doubloons, pearls, and rubies raced through his head. He took a deep breath, then grabbed hold of the handle and pulled.

Brian gasped.

Kermit jumped as though he had seen a ghost. Staring up at them from a bed of excelsior was a skull. A huge human skull.

"Don't touch it!" a sharp voice commanded. "Don't lay a finger on those bones."

7

Herbert Bender's Bones

Kermit looked from the hollow eyes of the skull into the twitching eye of Mr. Smith. The stranger stepped through the cellar door and knelt, almost reverently, before the metal box. "So you found them," he murmured. "Herbert Bender's bones."

Kermit looked at Brian, whose mouth had dropped open, then both boys took a step back. Mr. Smith lifted the skull gently out of the excelsior and turned it this way and that. It was enormous with a heavy ridge overhanging the eye sockets and a powerful, jutting foreface. Kermit stared wordlessly from the skull to the rapt expression on the stranger's face. Then he nudged

Brian in the ribs and nodded toward the cellar stairs. That was all Brian needed. He tore wildly up the steps with Kermit at his heels. They slammed the door shut behind them and clicked the lock shut.

"The other door!" Without pausing for a second, the boys tore out of the house and around the corner. The cellar door was still wide open, and Mr. Smith could be seen kneeling right where they had left him, as they slammed it shut and slid the bolt into place.

"Do you think . . ." Brian began in a shaky voice. "Do you think those bones are really . . ."

"Don't say it," Kermit interrupted. He could feel his heart beating like a kettledrum in his chest.

Brian looked soberly at the cellar door. "I think I'd better get Sergeant Toohill."

This time Kermit made no objections. The sooner the policeman got here the better. He ran to the dock with Brian and shoved the boat off. "I'll go get Mrs. Bender," he called as Brian began to row with all his might. "And hurry!"

He flew up the steps from the dock in a few bounds and set off through the trees to the end of the island. "Mrs. Bender," he called, but his voice came out so low and quavery he had to try again. "Mrs. Bender." He managed to sound a little more normal. "Where are you?"

"That you, Kermit?" her cheery voice came back. "I'm down here."

Kermit climbed down a small gully that led into the lake. Mrs. Bender was busily cutting through the undergrowth with her pruning shears. "Haven't found anything, have you?" she said, looking up from her work.

"We . . . that is . . ." Kermit stammered. He felt all shaky inside, and somehow his tongue just wouldn't form the words. How could he say—we found a box of bones—especially if they were really . . . but Kermit didn't even want to think about that possibility. "We've got a man locked in the cellar," was what came out when he finally got his tongue untwisted.

The old woman dropped her pruning shears. "Smithers!" she exclaimed so violently that the straw hat almost bounced off her head.

"No, Smith," Kermit corrected.

"Smith? So, that's what he's passing himself off as." Mrs. Bender scrambled out of the gully and brushed past Kermit like a hurricane in full

force. "That no-good," she raged, heading for the house. "Has he seen them?"

Kermit was taken aback. "Well . . . yes," he replied, struggling to keep up.

"Humph!" Mrs. Bender opened the front door and swept across the living room. "Quick thinking, locking him in." She had her hand on the cellar door.

"You're not going down there!" Kermit cried. "I mean, he could be dangerous. Brian went for Sergeant Toohill."

"Dangerous!" Mrs. Bender snorted, flinging open the door. "A miserable coward like Harry Smithers!" She stormed down the stairs and there was nothing for Kermit to do but follow. After all, he couldn't leave her alone and defenseless—even if she didn't *look* any more vulnerable than a battleship with all guns manned.

The stranger hadn't moved from the spot where the boys had left him. He was still holding the skull in one hand, and in the other he held a forceps-like instrument. He was just about to fit it around the skull, when Mrs. Bender charged across the cellar floor.

"Give me that," she demanded, making a grab for the skull.

"Mrs. Bender, if you please!" Smith or Smithers, or whatever his name was, held the skull out of her reach. His eye twitched nervously at the

corner, but his voice was calm. "I think I am more qualified than you to handle this."

"Well, I never . . ." Mrs. Bender sputtered, but she stood back as the stranger fitted the instrument over the skull, read some numbers from it, and jotted them down in a notebook.

Kermit watched in astonishment. He had never felt so confused. Mr. Smith was really Mr. Smithers, the treasure was a box full of bones, and the thief wasn't stealing them. He was . . . Kermit watched as Smithers fitted the instrument over the skull once again . . . he was measuring

it, he decided, as the man placed the skull gently
which was carefully buried in the excelsior.
back in the box and extracted a long, thick bone
"Now I think you've gone far enough!" Mrs.
Bender exclaimed. "Those are Herbert's bones
and, as his widow, I should be able to say who sees
them and who doesn't. I demand that you give
them to me." She stepped boldly forward and this
time she actually did grab one end of the long
bone.

The stranger looked surprised and then shocked
as he tightened his own grip on the bone. "Mrs.
Bender, please!"

"Don't you please me," she cried and gave the
bone a sharp jerk.

"Think what you're doing."

"Think!" she sputtered. "I'll thank you to
think." Her huge straw hat fell off her head, and
Kermit saw her draw back her foot to kick the
stranger in the shin. He closed his eyes. He felt
like he was watching one of those nutty movies
they show at kiddie matinees.

Just as Mrs. Bender's toe struck sharply against
the stranger's leg, Kermit heard a heavy step on
the cellar stairs and then a big voice boomed out.
"All right, what's the trouble here?"

"Sergeant Toohill, you're a police officer," Mrs. Bender cried. "Arrest this man."

"A police officer?" the stranger repeated in wonder, for the sergeant was dressed in an old plaid shirt and worn trousers. He had his badge pinned to his breast pocket, though, and he reached for his wallet to show his indentification.

"It's his day off," Brian hissed into Kermit's ear. "That's how we got here so fast. He was fishing on the lake in his motorboat."

Sergeant Toohill presented his identification to the stranger. "But I'm not arresting anybody until I find out what's going on around here. First, I'll take that." He indicated the bone that Mrs. Bender and the stranger still held. The stranger relinquished his hold at once and Mrs. Bender rather sheepishly handed it to the sergeant.

Kermit noted admiringly how the police officer took it without so much as blinking an eye. He didn't think he would have been so steady if someone had handed him a leg bone.

"And now, just who are you?" Sergeant Toohill addressed himself to the stranger.

"Dr. Harold Smithers. I am an anthropologist of some renown."

"Of some renown!" Mrs. Bender interrupted. "Harry Smithers, you're nothing but . . ."

"Please, Mrs. Bender," Sergeant Toohill warned.

"All right, I'll keep quiet," she grumbled. "But just ask him what he's doing here."

"That's exactly what I plan to do. Well, Dr. Smithers?"

Kermit and Brian leaned forward eagerly to hear the man's reply. "I only wanted to inspect Herbert Bender's bones," he declared. "But now" —he shook his head and threw up his hands in despair—"the whole thing has turned into a farce. Believe me, my intentions were entirely honorable, though my means, I admit, were a bit underhanded."

"Underhanded! I should say so!" Mrs. Bender exploded, but at a sharp glance from Sergeant Toohill, she quickly subsided.

The sergeant looked at the bone he held in his hand. "Herbert Bender's bones?" he repeated.

"Please, let me explain," Dr. Smithers said. "You must admit, Mrs. Bender, that we do owe the officer and these bewildered boys here an explanation."

Mrs. Bender looked at Kermit and Brian, and

in spite of her anger, she smiled slightly. "They do look confused," she admitted.

"Then if you'll allow me." Dr. Smithers indicated the box of bones, and Sergeant Toohill and the boys drew closer. Kermit looked at the stranger, and somehow he didn't seem so scary any more. After all, he was an anthropologist and maybe even a college professor like Kermit's father. It was hard to believe that he could be a thief.

Dr. Smithers waited until his audience had gathered around and then he once again lifted the skull from the box. "This," he said, turning the bone admiringly in his hands, "may be one of the greatest anthropological discoveries of the century."

"Then you admit it!" exclaimed Mrs. Bender.

"I do," Dr. Smithers replied, "though there was a time when I was certain that they, and your late husband, Mrs. Bender, were a fraud. There was a time when I thought these were merely the bones of a common orangutan."

"Orangutan!" Mrs. Bender snorted.

"Then there aren't any gold doubloons," Brian said in a disappointed voice.

"Gold doubloons?" Mrs. Bender looked surprised.

Brian's cheeks became red with embarrassment. "Well, we thought . . . that is, Kermit said . . . ah, heck, we thought that maybe Mrs. Bender had some kind of treasure hidden down here," he blurted out.

"But this is a treasure," Dr. Smithers replied. "These are the bones of a completely new type of fossil man."

"And you were planning to steal them," exploded Mrs. Bender.

Dr. Smithers looked shocked. "Steal them! Why, that never occurred to me. I only wanted to be able to inspect them to determine for myself if they were genuine."

"Boy, we sure had you all wrong," Brian said, looking sheepishly at Sergeant Toohill. "I guess it was just another false alarm."

A slow grin had been spreading across the sergeant's face for the last few minutes, and now it turned into a big smile. He began to shake all over with suppressed laughter. "What would I do without my detective helpers?" he chuckled, looking at Brian and Kermit, who turned bright red. "Yes, sir, I spend the whole winter just waiting for the summer when these two characters are around to stir up some excitement."

Kermit looked down at his shoes. Sergeant Toohill's laughter was all he needed. They'd never live this down. No honor, no glory, and no reward. Probably no Flash either, he realized with a sinking sensation in his stomach. Just a bunch of stupid old bones.

"But I'm glad they were so alert." Dr. Smithers came to the boys' defense. "These bones are quite valuable and someone could have been stealing them. I certainly gave these boys plenty of room for suspicion. But you see, I didn't want Mrs. Bender to know I had followed her here. Knowing how she felt about me, I anticipated what her reaction would be, but I just had to see these bones before anyone else did. You see, I feel rather responsible for them."

"Of course, of course," Sergeant Toohill said more seriously. "The boys did just what they should have done. But I'd sure like to know more about this fellow." He looked at the bone he still held in his hand. "A fossil man, you say?"

"That's right," Dr. Smithers replied. "Similar, I believe, to the Australopithecine fossils Dr. Leakey has been discovering in Africa."

"You're a little late recognizing that," Mrs. Bender interjected.

"That I humbly admit," Dr. Smithers replied with a sigh. "Unfortunately an all too-common occurrence in science. You see"—he addressed himself once again to Sergeant Toohill and the boys—"many years ago, when I was young— and I am afraid rather arrogant—Herbert Bender brought these bones to me to examine in my capacity as an assistant director of the anthropology collection at the Smithsonian Institution.

"He was something of an amateur anthropologist, and his finding of the bones had received what I thought was rather undue publicity. The popular press was fascinated with the idea of a missing link between man and the apes, and that was exactly what Herbert Bender claimed he had found.

"I examined the bones and—hampered by my own preconceptions—decided they were nothing more than those of an orangutan—an ape native to the Malays where they were found. Granted they appeared to be in a fossilized state, but there had been hoaxes perpetrated before in which bones were treated to make them seem very old, and a hoax was what I deemed Herbert Bender and his bones to be. I refused to grant them any space in the collection—even as a gift—and what was more, I wrote a long article in an anthropological journal labeling Bender's bones a fraud."

"Poor Herbert," Mrs. Bender murmured. "He was so discouraged. No one would believe him."

"They didn't believe Galileo or Gregor Mendel, either," Brian said seriously.

Kermit looked at him in surprise. "How'd you know about those guys?" he asked. All Brian had ever seemed interested in was reading comics and taking machines apart to see how they worked.

"Just something my teacher mentioned," Brian mumbled, blushing till his ears were red.

"The young man is right," Dr. Smithers agreed. "Many great scientists and discoverers have been unappreciated in their own times. People remembered the Bender bones only when similar finds had been made in Africa. *The New York Times* recently wrote an article in which they mentioned Herbert Bender's unheeded discovery, and it was shortly before that that I asked Mrs. Bender if I might examine them again. I can hardly blame her for refusing."

Mrs. Bender fiddled absent-mindedly with her dangly necklace. She was obviously beginning to

think better of the anthropologist. "I just didn't want to see the whole thing repeated," she said slowly. "And besides, I didn't know myself where they were."

"You mean to tell me you didn't know they were buried down here?" Sergeant Toohill said.

Mrs. Bender shook her head. "No. The summer Herbert died, I was visiting my sister in Michigan. He must have hidden them while I was gone, meaning to tell me later, but he never got the chance."

The police officer scratched the back of his head thoughtfully. "Well, if they're as valuable as the doctor here seems to think," he said, "then this cellar is a mightly funny place to hide them."

"Not really," Dr. Smithers objected. "As you can see, Mr. Bender packed them carefully. This box is lead lined."

"So that's why it was so heavy!" Kermit exclaimed.

"Actually," the anthropologist continued, "the greatest risk to fossilized bones like these is being broken through careless handling. They seem to have survived this short burial in the cellar as well as they did the centuries they were buried in the earth of Malaya."

Sergeant Toohill looked again at the bone he still held in his hand. "This case certainly is the most unusual I've ever had to deal with," he said. "What do you plan to do with the bones now that you've found them?"

"Well, if Mrs. Bender agrees," Dr. Smithers replied, "I'd like to take them back to the Smithsonian to study them more closely. Then I'd like to write an article to make what amends I can to Mr. Bender's reputation."

"About time," Mrs. Bender said. Her feathers were still a bit ruffled, but she was looking at Dr. Smithers with a friendlier light in her eyes.

The anthropologist smiled. "And right now," he said, "I'd like to pay these boys a small salary —as research assistants. We would never have found the bones this soon if it hadn't been for them. What with thinking, and digging, and fishing me out of the lake, I think they've earned it," he said. He took two five-dollar bills from his wallet and handed one to Brian and one to Kermit.

"Golly, research assistants!" Brian exclaimed. "What do you think of that, Foxie?"

But Kermit didn't dare say a word. He was afraid if he opened his mouth, the only words that would come out would be Flash, Flash, Flash!

8
Flash

Kermit thought they would never get away from the island. Mrs. Bender insisted on feeding them cookies and lemonade, and Sergeant Toohill kept asking questions about fossil men. And Brian, despite Kermit's warning scowls, kept eating cookies and asking Dr. Smithers about anthropology.

"Cripes, Foxie, what's your hurry?" Brian demanded when the boys had at last succeeded in saying all their thank yous and good-bys and were headed for Mrs. Bender's boat dock. "We might never get another chance to talk to a guy like that."

"Foxie!" Kermit exploded. "Just call me that one more time and I'll . . ." He clenched his fist angrily, but then he noticed the grin on Brian's face.

Brian reached into his pocket and took out the five-dollar bill Dr. Smithers had given him. "You can borrow it," he said, "but you've got to let me help train him."

"Gee!" Kermit looked at the money in Brian's hands and then at his friend's smiling face. "You're the greatest," he said. "You're . . . ah . . . gee." He was too embarrassed to say more, but Brian seemed to understand. They took turns rowing and made the shore in record time. Brian knew, too, without a word being said, that Kermit would want to go to the kennel alone. "I'll tell your mom you'll be late," he said as Kermit took off on his bike. "And you've got to let me be the first to see him," he called.

Kermit's legs had never before worked so hard on the pedals. He practically flew over the six miles to the Belvedere Kennels, stopping only once, at the foot of the long gravel drive. He leaned on the handle bars, trying to get his breath, and looked up at the boxer painted on the kennel sign. Belvedere boxers, and the best one of all was his.

The kennel owner was cleaning one of the runs

when Kermit reached the top of the drive. "Hey, wait a minute," he called as Kermit raced by him, heading for the puppy run. A frown crossed his face as he set his broom aside and walked slowly to the wire enclosure.

"Where is he?" Kermit exclaimed. In a second, his eyes went over the five boxer puppies, and in a second he knew that Flash was not among them. He could feel a lump rising in his throat, but he swallowed it back.

"What happened to him, Mr. Taylor?" he asked as calmly as he could.

"What happened . . ." a puzzled expression came into the man's eyes. "Didn't you . . . I mean, haven't you . . ." He looked at Kermit's quivering lower lip. "Gosh, son, you're not supposed to be here," he said in an embarrassed voice.

Kermit could hardly believe it. He looked at the kennel owner. The man flushed and turned away. The lump in Kermit's throat got bigger as he ran blindly for his bike. "Wait, son . . ." he heard Mr. Taylor's voice call after him as he sped down the drive. "Let me explain!"

Explain! Kermit rounded the corner onto the main road as though he hadn't even heard the

man's voice. He was never going to trust anyone again. How could he do it? How could he sell Flash after he had promised? Flash! Kermit's eyes fogged over and he had to blink to see where he was going. Flash. He never wanted to see another dog again in his whole life.

He hardly knew how he reached the summer colony, but soon he was turning onto the dirt road and riding under the faded sign. He passed the Digby bungalow, glad that Brian wasn't in the yard. He didn't feel like talking to anyone. All at once he heard barking—shrill puppy barking. The

sound was coming from the direction of the Fox bungalow, and Kermit's heart sank when he heard it. His father must have gotten one of the puppies from Manley's Peach Farm. How could he face it now?

"Foxie!" Brian's voice called from behind the garage as he pulled up in the driveway. "Look at this!"

Kermit could feel the lump in his throat rising again as he stepped around the corner of the garage. And then . . . wham! A ball of wriggly, golden-brown puppy hit him in the stomach. It crouched, its little stump of a tail wagging furiously, its eyes black and shiny on either side of the white streak down its nose. Then it barked again and leaped up to lick Kermit with its wet, pink tongue. Flash!

"You seem to know each other." Mr. Fox came out of the house and smiled at Kermit and the puppy.

"Dad! How did you . . . I mean . . . How did Flash . . ."

"Mr. Taylor called from the kennel this morning after you'd left," Kermit's father explained. He stooped to rub Flash's ears. "It seems someone wanted to buy this fellow, but Mr. Taylor said you had to have first chance."

"Then he didn't forget."

"No, he didn't. But I'm sorry you had to go over there. Mr. Taylor called just a few minutes ago. He didn't know what to say to you because he thought Flash was supposed to be a surprise. You must have felt pretty bad."

"I sure did." Kermit grinned, but he was feeling so good now, with Flash in his arms, that he could hardly remember how he had felt riding down the drive from the Belvedere Kennels.

"I'm sorry you had to be hurt," Kermit's father said, "but you shouldn't have kept this dog business such a secret."

"But gosh, Dad," Kermit protested, "I didn't think you would ever . . ."

"Now hold on a minute. Don't go thinking this dog is a present. When your mother and I realized how much he meant to you, we decided you could have him. We paid Mr. Taylor the twenty dollars you agreed upon, but it's up to you to pay him the rest over the summer."

"Gosh, Dad." Kermit didn't know what to say. "I'll . . ."

"Brian!" Kermit was interrupted by a familiar

voice. "Brian, where are . . ." Barbie came around the corner of the garage and stopped dead in her tracks when she saw Flash.

"Oh no!" Brian groaned, putting his hand over his ears.

But Barbie did not scream. She didn't even whimper. She walked right up to the puppy and patted him on the head. "Nice doggy," she said. "Where did you get such a nice doggy?"

Brian said nothing as he let this new revelation sink in. Then he began to smile, and Kermit knew exactly what he was thinking. He suspected the Digbys would be making a trip to Manley's Peach Farm in the near future. "Barbie, old pal," Brian said, "you're all right." He was just about to clap the astonished girl on the back when Mrs. Fox came out the kitchen door. She looked bewildered.

"The strangest thing just happened," she said. "A reporter from *The Poughkeepsie New Yorker* just called. He said someone named Smithers had given him a tip—a hot tip, is what he called it— on a story. And he's on his way here now to interview Kermit and Brian. What in the world could it be about?"

The next fifteen minutes were the most confusing Kermit had ever spent as he and Brian tried to explain everything at once. His parents kept asking questions about Dr. Smithers and Mrs. Bender and anthropology, and Barbie kept saying, "You mean a real skull?" and Flash kept bounding from one person to another.

Kermit was almost glad when Mrs. Bigelow's old car pulled up in the driveway and she stuck her head out the window. But when he heard what she had to say . . .

"I was just on my way home," she called cheerfully, "and I wanted to remind you." Kermit looked at Brian and Brian groaned. "Five hundred worms by tomorrow. Nice big juicy ones."

SUSAN MEYERS grew up in New York and California. For the background of this book she has drawn on memories of childhood summers spent at her grandparents' summer home on Whaley Lake in New York state. The many islands on the lake seemed adventurously mysterious where anything could happen; and a private worm business she and her sister set up those summers provided the initial impetus for writing this story.

Mrs. Meyers now lives in Los Angeles with her husband and young daughter. This is her third book for young readers.

IB OHLSSON was born in Copenhagen, Denmark, and studied art at the Copenhagen School for Applied Arts. He now lives in Pelham Manor, New York, with his wife and young son, and keeps very busy working as an industrial designer and book and magazine illustrator.